Welcome to our Happy Story Garden!

Use the power of your imagination and
dive into this magical world today!

Zinaida Kirko

DREAM WORLD

"In life, my dear, everything is like in a dream," said the captain, sharply turning the steering wheel, "but in a dream, everything is like in life - a dark moment inevitably follows a bright one! And you will not have time to blink an eye, as the world will turn upside down or from head to foot."

Chapter 1

The day it all started

On that day, the 30th of November, they woke up, as usual, in their beautiful huge house on Rose Street. All of its three floors were made of white bricks. When it snowed in winter, the place seemed to be invisible. But not for everyone.

"Look," Gladys pointed towards the garden, "someone is hiding there!"

She and Peter often sat in the attic and counted the passers-by if there was nothing better to do.

"There's no one there," the boy replied, looking closer.

A child screamed from below.

"She's crying again," Peter muttered.

He was eight years old. Gladys had just turned seven, and their little sister Maya was only a year old. Peter was the oldest child in the family. Dad kept saying that he had to take care of his sisters. And he didn't like the idea of that at all.

"No one's there," Peter repeated.

"I'm telling you, there is!" Gladys insisted.

It may have seemed to her, but a little man was hiding there, among the bushes.

She remembered how her mother had always told her about gnomes hiding in the gardens.

"It's a gnome," she said firmly, immediately adding it to the count.

"You can't count gnomes," Peter was indignant, "they don't exist!"

"No, they do exist!"

"Do not! Liar, liar pants on fire!"

And the children began to swear and fight, as was so often the case. They were screaming so loudly that their mother came up to them.

"What's happening?" she asked, rocking little Maya.

"He called me a liar," Gladys complained.

"Yes, and a sneak," Peter added and stuck out his tongue at his sister.

"Why are you arguing this time?" Mother sighed.

"He said gnomes don't exist," Gladys said, beginning to sob.

"Of course they do! In addition to gnomes, there are many different creatures in the world. You can't see them, but if they overhear you swearing, they can use their magical powers to punish you."

"And how will they do it?" Peter asked.

"They will be able to make all your dreams come true. Both good and bad. Therefore, you need to be careful."

She kissed the children and left.

Peter and Gladys looked at each other in disgust. They didn't speak to each other until evening. But right after dinner, they had a new quarrel. Peter found a spider and scared Gladys with it and then Maya. Both girls screamed until Dad threw it out.

"Didn't you hear what mother said?" Asked Gladys. "Magical creatures will punish you!"

"They will grant my wishes," said Peter, "which is exactly what I need!"

He made a face and ran to his room.

When the children fell asleep, everything was still on Rose Street. But during the deepest part of the night, a little man emerged from the bushes exactly where Gladys had pointed during the day. He was shortly followed by another one. They were no taller than the knees of any of the children. They were not gnomes but erlins from the magical world of dreams.

"Are you sure this is the right house?" one of them asked.

"Oh, yes," answered the second, "The astrologer pointed to it."

Both men rose into the air and flew to the window of the children's bedroom. And then they flew inside and hung in the air.

"Yes, yes, they are," said his friend.

Then the first erlin took out a bag and sprinkled the children with sparkling dust. Peter sneezed, Gladys tossed and turned in her sleep, and Maya woke up and laughed merrily, reaching out to the little men. But they had already disappeared.

The following day, the children, as per habit, woke up, washed, and went down to breakfast. However, instead of the pleasant smell of toast and fried eggs, their mother's smile, and their father's greeting, they were met by their parents' white-as-a-sheet chauffeur. He demanded that they get into the car as soon as possible.

The children had no choice but to follow him. As they were leaving, they saw through the window how their beautiful town was being destroyed right in front of them. The houses' walls were crumbling, the roofs were falling, and the streets were changing their direction.

Of course, Maya was only a year old, and she hardly understood anything, but Peter and Gladys were terribly upset. They have been away from home before. To their grandmother for the summer or Aunt Elsa for the weekend for instance. But on those occasions, there wasn't the chaos they were seeing now.

"What's happening?" Peter asked in annoyance, who had realised that he would now not be able to play his favourite video games.

"Hard times have come," the driver answered in a trembling voice. "Inexplicable destruction is taking place in the world! Your parents will return as soon as they can. And I have to take you to a safe place."

Gladys shuddered as she saw the wall of the house they were passing fall down. Destruction was everywhere. The ugly ruins of once beautiful buildings were now visible everywhere you looked, with pillars of swirling dust rising to the sky.

Gladys closed the window and turned to Peter.

"Come on, stop thinking only about yourself," she said. "Don't you care what happened to our parents?"

"My only concern is that now I will not be able to play and do what I want anymore!" the boy answered so loudly that Gladys flinched, and little Maya began to cry.

"You see what you've done," Gladys said, calming her. "Don't cry. Soon the parents will come back for us."

The car made a sharp turn, dodging falling trees. And they almost fell, barely holding on to each other.

This went on for quite some time until they left the city. And then the world plunged into darkness. The children began to nod off and soon fell asleep.

They woke up only when the driver opened the door and loudly called their names in an anxious voice. When they opened their eyes, they felt cold and damp, and huge drops of rain drummed on the roof of their large car.

"Come on, get out," he demanded, "you'll be safe here."

Gladys took Maya in her arms and followed Peter, who got out of the car in annoyance.

In front of them was a vast dark building with warped turrets and stairs. It looked as though it had been added to and rebuilt many times.

A hunched old man with an oil lamp in his hand was approaching along the long, curved path.

"Ahhh, new arrivals," he said, breaking into a crooked smile that made the children numb with shock. "Welcome to Sunfield, an orphanage for especially naughty children!"

And he laughed so loudly that he drowned out the sound of the rain.

"Shelter?" Peter was indignant, "Why won't they take us to my aunt or... well, at least to someone else! We have many relatives!"

"Because great destruction has come," answered the chauffeur, "and nowhere will you be better cared for than here in Sunfield. That's what your parents decided."

And he drove away, leaving them alone with the old man, who wandered towards the entrance, still laughing. The children had no choice but to follow him.

They thought it couldn't get any worse. But when they got closer, the door opened, and a formidably large overweight woman appeared on the threshold.

She immediately looked at them sternly.

"Bargo, who are these untidy, unwashed, and unkempt children?" she asked.

"The next orphans," the old man answered with a groan and turned off the lamp, "there will be many of them now!"

"Can anyone explain to us what is going on here?" Peter exclaimed impatiently.

The woman's eyebrows arched and merged into a " V ".

"How dare you scream in this place!" she hissed at him, "when everyone else has long been asleep!"

"Hush, Marpel," the old man soothed her. "The children just want to know what happened to their world," he turned to them, "and I will tell them!"

Bargo extended his hooked finger, which spiralled, and poked the boy's shoulder.

"And it happened that terrible things began in the world! Our whole world is now being destroyed every day, and nothing can be done about it. Only here in Sunfield you are safe, so you have no choice but to accept your fate and follow Aunt Marpel's orders!"

Little Maya, who understood something terrible was taking place, began to cry again, and Gladys began to calm her down.

"Come on," said the woman, "march to wash and sleep! Otherwise, you will be washing dishes in the kitchen all night!"

They had to wash in a cold bath in ice water with a bar of soap that smelled awful. But it was not as scary as a huge sleeping room, with sagging beds, under which rats ran and rustled. As soon as their heads touched the pillows, they heard a continuous rustling and became more scared than ever. But soon, sleep overcame them as it had been a long day.

However, in the middle of the night, Gladys awoke to a strange noise. She sat up in bed and looked around her. Everyone was asleep. Maya was no longer in the next bed.

"Maya," Gladys called.

She saw the girl walking towards her, and a transparent spirit with huge sad eyes was flying behind her.

"Who are you?" Gladys asked the apparition, taking Maya in her arms.

My name is Tobo. I am the keeper of Sunfield.

Gladys looked around to see if anyone else could see him, but the rest of the children were either quietly asleep or tossing and turning. But the strangest thing was that a chain was attached to the ghost's leg, which stretched to the ceiling and disappeared into it. Gladys reached out her hand, trying to reach Tobo, but he immediately vanished into thin air and reappeared to the side.

"You can't touch me," he said, "because I don't exist. I am from another world, the world of dreams."

"So, you're dreaming of me?"

"Maybe, maybe not." Tobo swirled in the air and smiled.

"Can you help me break this chain," he said, pointing to her, "so I can return to my world?"

"But how?"

"Using your imagination. Imagine that it breaks."

Gladys tried, but it didn't work.

"I can't," she replied.

"No one ever succeeds," the spirit answered sadly and sighed.

"Why are we here?" Gladys asked, "Why are we and all these children here?"

"The world began to collapse because people began to quarrel too often. But your parents took care of you," Tobo answered, "they knew that Sunfield was an enchanted place. Destruction will never touch it," he lowered his voice to a whisper, "because Sunfield is the door between worlds. The world of reality and the world of dreams."

Gladys didn't know what that meant.

"Is it possible to stop the destruction?"

"Of course, for this, you need to master your imagination to perfection. However, no one has succeeded here yet."

Tobo flickered, now disappearing, then reappearing.

"Help us," Gladys asked. "We must stop the destruction and return to our parents."

The ghost smiled sadly.

"You can change something only by sneaking into the Dream World. The door to it opens once on the longest night of the year, which will come tomorrow. But once you get there, you put yourself in great danger and may never return!

"All the same," Gladys answered," we can't sit idle! How can we find this door?"

"Oh," said Tobo, "you can hardly do that. But if you want to try it, follow the trail of ghosts to the Eternal Tree on Crooked Hill. "

"But you need to get there by midnight and return by dawn. If you don't get back in time, you will turn into a dream, like everyone who tried to do this before you! And if you go back and master your imagination to perfection, poor Tobo will finally be free!"

With these words, he disappeared, and silence returned. It took Gladys a long time to fall asleep, and when she did, she had weird dreams about a world that would never be the same again.

Chapter 2

Ghost Footprints

In the morning, the children were made to wash and comb their hair until every strand lay perfectly. Gladys looked at herself in the mirror.

There was not a single wrinkle in her pressed black dress, and her long curls were plaited into a tight braid. At first, she was upset, but when she turned around, she saw that all the girls in Sunfield looked like this.

Even little Maya was dressed and had her hair arranged like everyone else.

When she saw Peter, she was even more surprised. He had never been so neat and handsome. But the boy was angry and did not pay any attention to his sister.

When they entered the dining room, they saw that everyone around them was just as sad and upset.

"A cursed place," the boy exclaimed. "Tonight, I must run away from here!"

"But where will we go?" Gladys was confused.

"We? Who said we? I will go alone!"

"No, you won't! While my parents are gone, I am in charge here and will decide!"

"What?! Are you in charge? It's me who is in charge! I'm older!"

"So what!"

Maya looked from one to the other in surprise.

"If you're the one in charge, you should take care of us!"

"And I'll do it!"

And while Peter was realising what he had said, the teachers approached them and threw down plates of food in front of them. It was a thin, tasteless gruel that didn't look edible in the slightest.

"So we'll run away together?" Gladys asked, picking at her plate with a spoon.

"We have to," Peter muttered.

"I have a plan."

Gladys told them everything that happened to her at night.

"Trail of ghosts?" Peter chuckled. "You dreamed it!"

"What if I didn't? What if we can find them, get into the Dream World, and stop the destruction?"

Peter thought for a second. After all, there was nowhere to run from Sunfield. Indeed, destruction was everywhere. The only right decision was to try to stop them.

"Well," he said," we will look for the trail of ghosts, "but if we don't find any, I will run away from here tomorrow without you!"

After breakfast, the three of them went to wander around the house.

They looked into every corner of each room, walked around the entire courtyard and garden and even visited the roof. But a whole day passed, and they still did not find anything.

Peter was angry with his sister, and they ate in silence.

"I will never believe in your fiction again," he said at last.

"I did not make up anything," Gladys protested. "If you do not want to come with us, I will continue the search myself."

"That's great, and in the meantime, I'll devise a plan to escape from here alone!"

They were continuing their arguing when they suddenly heard Maya's surprised scream. Both immediately turned to her. The girl squeaked happily and pointed at her plate. And there, one could see a small shape resembling a footprint.

"Ghost trail!" Peter exclaimed.

It shimmered like Tobo did last night, and the children did not doubt they had found what they were looking for.

"And you said that this is nonsense!" Gladys was offended.

But Peter was already examining the floor and noticed a new footprint in the distance.

"They're everywhere!"

Gladys took Maya in her arms and ran after her brother.

There were many tracks. They sometimes gathered together, then dispersed, and sometimes they led to the ceiling and disappeared into the corners.

- What are you doing here? It's time for you to sleep! Marpel suddenly appeared menacingly and put her hands on her hips, preventing the children from passing.

- We ... we ... - Gladys did not know what to come up with.

"We're lost and don't know where the bedroom is," Peter replied.

- Really?! Or maybe you're just hanging around here doing nothing because you're naughty little kids?!

The fat woman moved threateningly at him, but Peter didn't flinch or even look away.

- March to bed! And I don't want to see you here! Marpel screamed.

The children had no choice but to go towards the sleeping room. But as soon as they took a few steps, Maya squealed again, pointing to a new string of footprints.

"They lead to the basement," whispered Gladys.

The children stopped at the entrance. It was damp and dark below, and only the flickering of footprints illuminated their path. Gaining courage, Peter took the first step and the girls followed him.

They walked for a long time, looking at the intertwining footprints on the floor, walls, and ceiling. It seemed that crowds of ghosts that they did not see were going somewhere to gather all together.

The children came to a small hatch in the floor, on which there were many footprints, and stopped. Peter opened it and was about to climb inside, but Maya became scared and burst into tears.

"Let's wait," said Gladys, comforting the little one.

"Wait? Until fat Marpel comes here? No! You can stay here if you like, and I'll go alone."

With those words, Peter disappeared into the darkness, and Gladys was left alone with Maya crying in her arms. Both of them were scared, but they could not turn back.

Suddenly, a light came on in the distance. Gladys turned around. In the darkness, she saw old Bargo approaching them. The girls had no choice but to crawl through the hatch and slam it shut.

As soon as they took the first step, the floor collapsed. They slithered down a dark tunnel strewn with shimmering footprints.

It wasn't long before they fell to the ground. Maya laughed and squealed with joy, but Gladys was not laughing. She looked around. Even though they fell downwards for only a short time, the world seemed to turn upside down. They were on a hill, and in the distance, they could see the crooked building of Sunfield.

"Peter!" Gladys exclaimed, looking around, but he was nowhere to be found.

"Ahhh, you are looking for a naughty boy," she heard a voice behind her and turned around.

In front of her was a huge tree, as powerful and ancient as the girl had ever seen. One could see a wrinkled face with huge wise eyes in its thick trunk. The tree twirled its winding branches and smiled slyly.

"If you're looking for the angry one, you'll most likely never find him again!" the tree laughed.

"Peter is our brother," exclaimed Gladys, and Maya squeaked menacingly, "and we must find him at all costs."

"Hmm..." said the tree, "then it's too late because he disappeared inside dreams, and finding him would be the same as finding the sun at night."

Gladys looked around again.

"I think I understand," she said, looking at Sunfield and the fields below. "We are on Crooked Hill, and you... you are the Eternal Tree!"

The tree smiled broadly and bowed, creaking its thick branches, from which colourful birds flew out with cries.

"I've been standing here for ages and rarely have guests. They all come here with selfish goals and demand the impossible from me. Here you are; why did you come here?"

"We have followed the trail of the ghosts to enter the dream world and stop the destruction, but first, we need to find our brother."

"Well, hmm... hmm... for that, all three of you must give me the most precious thing you have."

But Gladys didn't know what it could be. Her pockets were empty, and little Maya was too small to possess anything.

"Take what you want," said the girl, "just help us."

"Hmm," the tree smiled again, "so be it."

And, lifting the thick branches, it laughed with a terrifying laugh. In the next moment, thousands of ghosts moved towards them from different directions, eclipsing everything around them. Gladys held Maya close to her. Together, they swirled in a whirlwind that carried them away in an unknown direction.

Chapter 3

City of Dreams

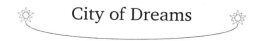

When Gladys opened her eyes, everything was bright and sunny. She was in a park surrounded by high mountains and could see a city in the distance.

She did not immediately understand what had happened but noticed two old people next to her. One was so ancient that his beard coiled three times around the bench on which he sat. And an old woman with a wrinkled face sat nearby on the ground and played with it.

"Maya!" called Gladys.

To her surprise, the old woman smiled and walked over to her.

Gladys backed away and fell. She looked at her feet and was horrified at the sight. They were old and wrinkled.

"Peter!" the girl called.

The old man looked up at her with a frown.

"Is that you, Gladys?"

He stood up and shuffled towards her.

"I thought it was all your fault!"

"My fault?!"

"Yes, it was you who gave the Tree years of our lives, and now we will die of old age any minute!"

"But I didn't know," the girl was upset, "besides, I had to find you."

"To find me? Like I couldn't manage myself!"

"Of course not," they suddenly heard someone's voice, "you would have disappeared into dreams, and if not for the girl, you would have never returned!

The old people turned around. In front of them was a small man with a cane. He was short with a very wide smile and cheerful, wise eyes.

"Who are you?" Peter yelled at him.

"My name is Jolo," the little man answered. "I am an erlin, the collector of dreams."

"Collector of dreams?" Gladys was surprised. "Did we really get into the world of dreams?"

"Of course you did! However, you are unlikely to be able to get out, even before dawn, especially since you are quarrelling, as it does not befit a brother and sister at all."

The old men looked at each other.

"Help us," Gladys pleaded, "we've come to stop the destruction. And we can't do it without your help!"

Jolo laughed, clutching his stomach.

"Stop destruction!" he repeated. "No one has succeeded yet! However, till dawn, you are guests of this world, so I will help you."

And, waving his hand to them, he went to the city, visible ahead. And the three aged children followed him.

They walked slowly, stumbling and supporting each other. And the erlin, smiling, walked forward and hummed a song under his breath.

Soon, they approached a town with small multi-coloured houses, the roofs twisted up in bizarre spirals, and the walls were higher than one another. Doors and windows were slanted and bent, shaking and changing their shape.

"What an amazing city!" Gladys was surprised.

"I see nothing amazing about it," Peter muttered.

"This is the Dreamarium, the city of dreams where we collect them piece by piece," Jolo said proudly.

He led them through one of the crooked doors into a red house. The old men had to bend double to get into it. There were a lot of erlins inside, who waved their hands in greeting.

"At night, we erlins visit people and collect their feelings and emotions, and then bring them here and sort them to create new dreams."

The old people saw a long conveyor stretching in front of them, along which various objects moved.

"Fears, happiness, frights, joys," Jolo pointed at them, "they all belonged to someone and will soon become someone's dreams, and here," he said and led them through the narrow door to the next house, "we are testing dream fragments."

He took a small vial from many of the same vessels that stood everywhere and splashed it into the air. The next moment, the old children felt the sea air and found themselves on the beach, building sandcastles. However, the vision immediately disappeared.

"If you're so omnipotent," Peter said, "create a dream where we're young again with our parents in a world without destruction and leave us there forever."

The erlins all around laughed and giggled. Jolo turned to the old man, and his face became sad.

"Alas," he said, "dreams are fleeting and short-lived. They disappear as soon as they appear. And we don't create them. This is done by the Dream Master Illusius. However, I can help you."

"How?" Gladys was surprised.

"I can take the experiences throughout your lives to create new dream fragments from them. Then you will become children again."

With these words, he touched them with his cane, pulling out multi-coloured threads from them. In less than a minute, the old people turned into children again.

Gladys and Peter could not get enough of looking at each other, and little Maya squealed, demanding to be picked up.

Suddenly there was a loud, terrifying rumble, and all the erlins rushed out. The houses immediately began shaking. The shutters closed. An icy wind blew from all sides. The clouds thickened in the dark sky, and the sun, which had shone brightly before, disappeared as if it had never been there.

"Hide," Jolo shouted.

And they hid in the basement of one of the houses. The children clung to the small window, looking out at the coming storm. Goosebumps ran down their skin from fear. Many ominous ghosts flew out of the dark cloud. They circled over the city and flew inside every house.

"What are those?" Peter asked.

"These are the most evil of all the spirits known to the world," Jolo whispered, "they select all the bad emotions and fears we have found to create the worst of dreams that will torment and drive people crazy!"

Maya cried. Jolo slammed the window shut and covered it with a wooden plank.

"Be sure they do not find you. Otherwise, your lives will always be filled with horrors!"

He sat down at a table with easy chairs, poured tea into painted cups, and then tapped them with his magic cane.

"Drink, this is the tea of sweet dreams. It will help you calm down."

The kids immediately sat down and drank a tea that made them feel so good that even Peter broke into a smile.

"But why do these spirits terrify people if dreams are created by the Dream Master Illusius?" Gladys asked.

"It's not that simple," Jolo replied.

He looked at them as if he didn't dare tell them a secret but then changed his mind and banged his cane on the table.

"Okay, I see that you have come with a great intention to stop the destruction, so I will tell you what I know."

And, having settled down in a comfortable chair, he began his story.

"Once upon a time... a very long time ago, there was a vast city in the Dream World with tall majestic buildings that touched the sky.

It was called the City of Tall People because great people lived there, each five or even ten times taller than any of you. And these people were Dreammakers. They created dreams of incredible beauty where anyone could get lost and forget themselves.

They mastered their imagination so well that they could change reality however they wanted. And nothing was impossible for them.

But one day, for unknown reasons, these people... disappeared!

Dissolved in the air, leaving their city, which decayed and collapsed every day until only ruins remained. At that time, out of nowhere appeared Cornelius, a great follower of the Dreammakers, who claimed to have mastered their art. However, this was different. He could only create dreams, not change reality.

For many years, he created dreams for people until old age overtook him. It was then that he took the boy Illusius as an apprentice. I don't know where he found him, but they say he was the last of the Tall Men. Cornelius taught him everything he knew. Everything would have been fine, but Cornelius was tormented by the fact that he could not change reality, and day after day, he forced Illusius to conduct experiments with dreams. Once... as a result of such an experiment, the evil spirit Mortus broke free and seized power over all the horrors and fears of people. Cornelius died of old age and grief, and the young Illusius could never stop the evil that had appeared in the world. Because of this, people in the world began to quarrel too often. Therefore, our world began to collapse like yours, and no one can prevent this.

"So it's all Illusius's fault!" Peter said.

"No, Mortus is to blame!" objected Gladys. "So we must stop him!"

"But what can you three children do?" Jolo said, spreading his hands.

He opened the basement doors and climbed out. The sky was clear again. The sun shone brightly, and there was no trace of evil spirits.

"If you are not afraid," Jolo said, "then go beyond the distant horizon to the city of Tall People. There you will find Illusius. But you must head home because it will be dawn soon. If you fail, you could turn into dreams before you arrive."

With these words, he, singing a song, went back to the city of crooked coloured houses and soon disappeared behind one of the slanting doors.

Chapter 4

The Last Dreammaker

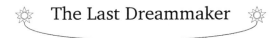

The children were walking down the road when Peter suddenly stopped.

"Dawn is coming," he said, "so the erlin is right, and we need to go home."

"But we won't get a second chance," Gladys objected, "besides, we still have time."

Maya pointed her little hand towards the boy and said something he couldn't understand.

"All right," he agreed, "but I will take the lead."

And he went forward in search of the far horizon, and Gladys and Maya followed him. But time passed. One road followed another, but the horizon did not get closer. Gladys saw Peter frowning and angry but decided not to argue with him.

"Look," he suddenly exclaimed, "this is what we need."

Ahead, giant balloons rose into the air. They were of various colours and sizes and, gleaming in the sun, went beyond the horizon.

As the children approached, they saw many strange creatures loading boxes and bags into baskets tied to the ground.

They were short and powerfully built, with hairy arms and legs, and long ears. They had large, clear blue eyes, with which they looked through binoculars. They appeared to be constantly on the lookout for something in the distance.

Noticing the children, the creatures immediately surrounded them.

"How interesting! Wonderful! Incredible!" they repeated.

"Who are you?" finally asked one of them, wearing a red hat.

"I'm Peter, and this is Gladys and Maya," the boy answered. "We are looking for Illusius to stop Mortus and the destruction in our world. And who are you?"

"Stop Mortus?! Awesome! Marvellous!" the creatures exclaimed.

"I'm Varius," the creature in the red hat replied, "and these are my Idea Gatherer friends. We travel through well-forgotten dreams to find ideas to help people, then send them to Illusius to implement them into new dreams."

"How interesting!" exclaimed Gladys. "Could you take us with you? We really, really need to talk to Illusius."

The idea collectors looked at each other and nodded in agreement.

"Of course, we can take you with us," Varius replied, "we were just on our way to Illusius to bring him a fresh batch of ideas!"

And he invited the kids to one of the air balloons. It was the largest and most beautiful of all. The children climbed into the basket, which rose high into the sky, revealing a view of the vast world of dreams.

"Wow," Peter exclaimed, turning to Varius, "I want to stay here and travel through my dreams with you!"

But Varius shook his head, turning the steering wheel sharply to the side.

"Alas, if you do not return home before dawn to your world, you will all turn into dreams. Only Illusius can help you avoid this."

Suddenly, the sun disappeared behind the clouds, and the sky darkened. Thunder and lightning cut through the horizon, which was getting closer.

"Oh no!" exclaimed Varius. "These are the ghosts of Mortus! They've come to take the best of the ideas we've found and use them for their evil purposes!"

The children were horrified to find that scary ghosts were rushing towards them from all sides. Varius and the other idea collectors fought them off as best they could. They took out silver nets, threw them on the ghosts, and sprinkled them with silver dust. This made them dissolve and disappear into the air.

However, despite their best efforts, when the sun peeked through the clouds again, Varius found that at least half of the ideas he had been carrying were gone.

"And it happens every time," he said sadly. "If only you could stop Mortus, then the world could get all the ideas we find."

They floated through the air, crossing horizon after horizon until they reached the one farthest away.

"What is this?" Gladys asked, pointing down.

Before them were eerie ruins of large buildings. There were a great many of them, and they reached the heavens.

"This is the City of Tall People," said Varius, "this is where the great dreamers once lived."

The ball slowly sank to the ground, and Varius opened the door for the children.

"We've arrived," he said, "His house is on that hill over there."

The children looked where he pointed. Nearby, on a hill, was a massive house with intertwined turrets, ladders, entrances, and exits. It was the only intact building in the entire area.

"Be careful," Varius warned them, "don't be fooled when you go inside, or you might get lost in them forever!"

Peter immediately ran towards the house. Gladys thanked Varius and then followed him.

"It would be polite of you to thank the idea collectors," she said.

"You should thank me for bringing us here!" Peter said proudly.

Gladys sighed but said nothing. Maya made a long, disappointed sound.

As they approached, they discovered that around the house was a small garden with many strange-looking trees. They opened the carved gate and stepped inside.

As soon as they stepped onto the paved path, illusions approached them from all sides. In one of them, their friends called them to play. In the other - a house where their parents were waiting for them, and in the third, someone who called himself Illusius offered to fulfil all their cherished dreams.

"That's him," Peter said, "Illusius, we found him!"

But Gladys held her brother's hand.

"It's just an illusion," she replied, pulling him back.

The visions faded, and the children moved forward towards the entrance of the house. As they approached, they saw many stairs leading from one to the other. They wandered around for a long time until, finally, in despair, they sat down on the steps.

"What a stupid house," Peter muttered, "where the stairs don't lead anywhere!"

The children heard a soft chuckle.

"These stairs are alive!" exclaimed Gladys, standing up. "Perhaps you should politely ask them to guide us in the right direction."

"I'm not going to do that!"

"Then I'll do it!"

Gladys politely asked the stairs to guide her to Illusius. The steps immediately lined up in a row, opening the entrance to the carved doors. The girl stepped forward, but when she turned around, she saw that Peter was not behind."

"Peter!" she called. "Peter!"

There was no answer.

In a moment, she found that she and Maya were standing on a wide platform on the top floor.

A tall man in a long green suit appeared before them. He had huge black eyes full of sadness. He was twice the height of any other person, very pale and thin.

Many watches were sticking out of his pockets, which he constantly took out and checked as if worried about the time. Gladys also noticed that clocks were everywhere. They ticked, rang, or simply stood with seemingly frozen hands.

"Ah... guests," Illusius said, finally noticing the children, "I think there were three of you?"

"My brother, Peter, disappeared!" said Gladys. "I don't know where he is."

"Alas," the Dreammaker replied. "Even I don't know where he is. After all, impoliteness leads people to the most unpleasant places and situations."

Gladys and Maya looked at the clock as though spellbound.

"This is the time of human lives," he explained, "and here is yours."

He pointed to three clocks, the hands of which were approaching the inscription "dawn", after which there was nothing.

"Help us, I beg you," Gladys pleaded. "We must find Peter, stop the destruction in our world at all costs, and return home before dawn!"

"Great goals have brought you here," Illusius smiled, "but, alas, I cannot help you. However, I'm glad you stopped by to see me. I'm so alone!"

He sat down in an armchair with a terribly sad look and began to look at the horizon.

"But you are all-powerful," said Gladys. "You create dreams for the people of the whole world!"

"This is not enough!" Illusius said.

Suddenly, all the clocks chimed at once, and the Dreammaker jumped up as if he had been stung.

"It's time to create dreams!" he said, "and since you came to visit me, I'll show you how it's done!"

With these words, he raised his hands, and he, Maya, and Gladys found themselves among the ruins in the city of Tall People.

"Here," he said and handed Gladys a small transparent stone. "This is a shard of time. Look into it, and you will see what this great city once was!"

Gladys looked and saw the city as it was when the Tall Men lived in it. They walked and laughed while creating dreams and also changing reality as if it were a game.

"Wow!" the girl exclaimed.

"My teacher Cornelius said I am one of them," continued Illusius. "After all, I am as tall as they are and just as great! I have the skill to create great dreams!"

The next moment, Gladys saw Sunfield and how the children ran out in a crowd. There, they were being given sweets and toys from shops. Everything was free and in unlimited quantities. They were happy, and Gladys saw them smiling in their sleep.

36

The erlins stood next to them and collected their happy moments.

"You see, I give them joyful emotions and then collect their happiness for someone else."

And Gladys saw old people in a sparsely furnished house, sleeping peacefully and enjoying their sleep, where they were young again, dancing and singing with their family.

"I can create everything in the world," the Dreammaker continued.

And Gladys continued to see countless dreams crumbling into the world with multi-coloured pieces.

"However, this is not enough!"

"Why?" Gladys was surprised.

Suddenly, everything disappeared, and they were back on the roof with the clock ticking non-stop. Illusius became incredibly sad.

"Because," he replied, "I'll never be able to wake her up!"

He ran his hand through the air, and a long rope appeared before them, going from nowhere to nowhere. An incredibly beautiful crystal glass girl was dancing on it.

"Teacher Cornelius said that I can only become a true Dreammaker when I create the most beautiful dream that can wake up a dancing girl on a tightrope! However, no matter what I do, she won't wake up!"

Gladys looked at the girl, who, like a feather, whirled and danced on a thin line to music that no one could hear. Illusius seemed to be fascinated by her every movement.

"I believe that you can wake her," said Gladys. "You are a great Dreammaker! You must defeat Mortus and stop the evil in the world!"

"No," Illusius shook his head. "I tried for many years, but it's all hopeless."

And he sat down again in his chair, looking at her, and Gladys saw in his eyes the reflections of the infinite number of dreams that he was creating at that very moment.

Suddenly, Gladys noticed that Maya was disappearing into thin air. Then she looked down at her hands and saw that she was dissolving too. It was strange because they still had a few minutes before dawn broke. She began to call for help, but Illusius was so absorbed in the girl's dance on the rope that he did not hear them. They disappeared, and the platform with the clock of lives vanished as if it had never existed.

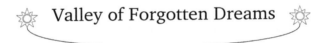 Valley of Forgotten Dreams

When Gladys opened her eyes, she found herself in the middle of a valley filled with various items of junk.

There was so much of it that it stretched like mountains to the horizon. The sun burned mercilessly, and the dry earth cracked from one touch. She was very thirsty.

A little girl was nearby, but Gladys could not remember her or herself. Taking her in her arms, she went forward in search of water. They reached a lake with tall trees and bushes growing nearby. Having drunk enough, they sat down on the ground. Everything around and the little girl seemed so familiar to Gladys, but she couldn't remember anything.

Suddenly, they heard screams in the distance.

"Help! Help!" someone floundered in the lake and called for help.

Gladys immediately rushed into the water and helped out. In front of her was a tiny creature. It was breathing heavily and grunting, clutching its stomach.

"Who are you, my saviours?" it asked breathlessly.

But Gladys could not answer, and Maya babbled something incomprehensible.

"Aaah," the creature said with understanding and shook its head. "You were bewitched by Mortus and placed in the valley of forgotten dreams."

"Mortus?" Gladys asked with surprise. "Who is that?"

"It doesn't matter," the creature replied. "What matters is that I'm Treya, a resident of the Valley of Forgotten Dreams, and I can help you. Many people think that once they see dreams, no one needs them anymore, but this is not so."

And she stepped forward through the rubble, signalling them to follow.

"So, these are all forgotten dreams?" Gladys asked, looking around."

"Yes," answered Treya. "Imagine! There are so many interesting things here!"

She stopped near a mountain where a small village came into view surrounded by more creatures like Treya. They were busy with work and did not pay attention to the guests.

"We collect the best parts of old dreams and send them to Master Illusius to create new ones."

"How interesting!" said Gladys. "But could you explain who we are and why we are here?"

"As I said," answered Treya, "you helped me, so I will help you".

They came to a massive pile of rubble, and Treya pulled a piece out.

"Your past life is nothing more than an old dream," she said, "now lying somewhere among this rubbish. Here, look!"

Gladys and Maya looked at the broken piece. It was a fragment of their past life when they walked and had fun with their parents.

Treya took another one. It was a fragment of their life in Sunfield. She took out more and more fragments. And gradually, the girls began remembering everything.

"What can we do?" Gladys exclaimed. "The dawn is approaching, and we still haven't stopped Mortus!"

"Nobody has been able to do this yet, so you better hurry and go back home," Treya waved her hand.

"But we can't go back without Peter," Gladys was upset. "We must find him before it's too late!"

The girl stood up, and a transparent stone fell out of the pocket of her dress.

"Amazing!" exclaimed Treya, picking it up. "It's a piece of time! With its help, you can see any moment of your past and even someone else's."

"Then we must find out where Peter has disappeared to!" Gladys said.

Together, they looked inside the fragment and saw the boy. He was in a large, crooked building in a spacious hall. Next to him was Mortus himself - an immense, ugly, hump-backed evil spirit.

"You did not come here by chance," said Mortus. "I have been waiting for someone like you for a long time. I will make you as powerful as Illusius if you become my apprentice!"

And Gladys and Maya were horrified to see Peter nodding in agreement.

"Look how beautiful it is to create horrors and nightmares and how beautiful it is to destroy!"

And Mortus began to give nightmares to the children of Sunfield. First, it was spiders and insects chasing them, then parents who scolded them, and then the orphanage walls began to crumble.

The boy laughed and rubbed his hands. And Mortus led him to the window, behind which a great multitude of evil ghosts and spirits waited in the darkness of the night.

"I have gathered a huge army. This day, we will defeat Illusius together, and you will create terrible nightmares for everyone in the world. In time, you will become even more powerful than me! Do you agree?"

Peter nodded again.

"If you are ready, here is your first task. You must send your sister to the valley of oblivion and never regret it!"

"Oh no!" Gladys exclaimed. "Peter did it! He sent us here!"

"What a mean boy," Treya said.

Even Maya shook her head in disapproval.

"No, you don't know Peter at all," Gladys protested, "at heart, he is very, very good!"

"Then why did he do that?"

But Gladys didn't know. She just sighed and stood up.

"We must head back to Illusius now and warn him of Mortus's plans!"

"And we must gather as many inhabitants of the world of dreams as possible to defeat the army of evil spirits!"

With these words, Treya climbed the mountain of debris and let out such a loud cry that she was heard in all parts of the world of dreams.

In the distance, Gladys saw airships approaching them, probably made from the wreckage of forgotten dreams. They creaked and rumbled but moved forward through the air and soon stopped near the girls.

"These are airships of the past. They will take you back to Illusius," Treya said, "and help delay the dawn."

"Thank you!" Gladys said. She took Maya in her arms and climbed aboard.

"Whatever happens, don't let Mortus take the Tall Men's medallion from Illusius. If he does this, all will be lost!"

Gladys nodded. On board, she was met by a smiling captain. His eyes reflected the experience of many years. He must have seen a lot in his lifetime.

"The weather is beautiful," he said, "not a single nightmare on the horizon!"

He lit an old long pipe, and Maya made a cheerful sound. And the airship took off into the sky.

"How can you be so calm, knowing what lies ahead of us?" Gladys asked.

"In life, my dear, everything is like in a dream," said the captain, sharply turning the steering wheel, "but in a dream, everything is like in life - a dark moment inevitably follows a bright one! And you will not have time to blink an eye, as the world will turn upside down or from head to foot."

He stopped near a giant clock hanging in the middle of the sky, jumped off the airship onto the clock and attempted to move the clock's hands.

"Come on, help me!"

Gladys joined him.

"Playing with time is no joke," said the captain, "but we are old friends, so no one will notice how I add just one extra hour to eternity," he jumped down and gallantly extended his hand to Gladys. "For you, I delayed dawn!"

45

They moved forward again, cutting through the clouds and circling the rainbow.

"So, you believe in our victory?"

"You see," said the captain. "In the world of dreams, everything depends on you, but in the real world, everything depends on the world of dreams. So, in the real world, everything depends on you. And you depend on the world of dreams. The main thing is not to get confused!"

Gladys thought it would be good to write it down so she could think about it later, but the captain continued.

"Be that as it may, I travel often and communicate with various passengers. So, one day, I was transporting a whole crowd of Dream Archivers. These guys know what's what and how things are. So, one of them told me that Illusius is indeed a descendant of the Tall People, and Mortus is a part of his power that he cannot control. And if Cornelius were alive, he would have told him about it."

"Why can't Illusius do that?"

"I don't know," the captain shrugged. "Maybe because he's too busy creating the perfect dream that doesn't exist. His ship is moving towards a target, which is too ghostly and incomprehensible."

They moored at the platform with the clocks. The girls said goodbye to the captain, who saluted them and then abruptly turned the helm and disappeared into the clouds.

Chapter 6

Battle

Gladys and Maya looked around - they were alone. They wandered around the area with the clocks of life but could not find Illusius.

And the crystal girl on the rope continued dancing to music no one could hear. Gladys found herself unable to take her eyes off her. So perfect and simple were her movements. But she remembered the coming battle and her brother in trouble.

"Illusius!" called Gladys, "Illusius!"

The Dream Master appeared in front of her. His eyes were even sadder than before.

"Ah, my new friends," he said, pulling a watch out of his pocket and comparing it with those everywhere on the platform.

"We have come to warn you," Gladys said excitedly. "A battle is coming, and Mortus is going to take over the Dream World."

"Oh, I don't like battles," answered Illusius and sat down in a chair, turning pale. "I am a creator, a man of art, and I don't understand anything about military affairs!"

"But you must try because if Mortus wins, there will be neither joy nor light left in the world. There will be only darkness and nightmares! By dawn, we will turn into dreams, and our world will collapse completely!"

49

Illusius covered his face with his hands.

"Then I must create the perfect dream as soon as possible!"

And he rose, stretching out his hands to the dancer and offering her the most beautiful of dreams. But she danced as before, paying no attention to him.

Gladys walked to the platform's edge and saw that a dark army of ghosts and evil spirits had gathered on the horizon, preparing to attack at any moment. But the most terrible thing was that Peter stood over them all with a pencil in hand.

"Illusius! Illusius!" the girl called again.

He turned and, seeing the army, let out a frightened cry. Then he raised the binoculars to his eyes and began to examine her.

"I see your brother holding a wishing pencil in his hands," he said, handing her a small pencil. "I will give you one too. Use it to create whatever you want! Perhaps you can hold on to them while I create the most perfect dream."

"But what should I do?" she asked.

"Use your imagination!" answered the Dreammaker.

Gladys took the pencil, and her hands trembled. After all, she never created anything. But now, looking at Illusius, who was busy creating the perfect dream, she knew she had no choice.

The girl drew a line, then another, and then another; she was getting the hang of it; the more she tried, the more she created! More and more creatures appeared right out of thin air, ready to protect them. And then many inhabitants of the world of dreams joined them.

There was Jolo with the erlins, Varius with the Collectors of Ideas, and Treya's followers from the valley of forgotten dreams. All of them were ready to defend their world.

Mortus himself appeared in the distance. He signalled, and the battle began. Ghosts circled, casting nightmares and horrors, but the creatures of the dream world repelled their attacks.

Gladys and Peter competed with each other, drawing more and more obstacles and creatures that immediately rushed to the attack. At first, the boy was winning because he could draw much better than Gladys, but soon, she got so good at it that she easily deflected any of his attacks.

Suddenly, Mortus walked up to Peter and said something to him. The boy grinned, creating a black lake, and Mortus filled it with nightmares. The lake grew and grew in size until it reached the edge of the life-clock tower.

One of the ghosts flew up to Gladys and pushed her down. But the girl managed to grab the edge. The wishing pencil went to the bottom, and there was nothing she could do. She saw Peter laughing in the distance. However, the next moment, the boy slipped and fell into the very depths of the lake.

"Peter!" shouted Gladys and immediately dived after him.

She was instantly surrounded by nightmares and horrors. She moved forward, searching for her brother, but alas, fear captured her so much that she was about to lose consciousness.

However, she reached the bottom and grabbed her brother's hand. The boy opened his eyes. Suddenly, someone forcefully pulled them both upstairs. Gladys turned around - it was Illusius.

He immediately dried up the lake of nightmares and entered the battle with Mortus. They hurled the most incredible dreams at each other.

"Peter!" Gladys called, "Peter!"

For a few moments, the boy stared ahead with glassy eyes. There was neither joy nor light in him. Suddenly, he woke up and, upon seeing Gladys, hugged her.

"Gladys," he said, sobbing, "Gladys, I've had terrible nightmares!"

"They are nothing," answered his sister. "These are just dreams."

"I will never again terrify other people," he said. "I hope you will forgive me for being impolite and offending you."

"Of course," Gladys said, hugging him. "But now we must hurry and help Illusius!"

They went towards the foot of the life-clock tower and saw Mortus ripping the medallion from Illusius's neck.

"Oh no!" exclaimed Gladys. "Not that!"

Illusius's strength was instantly exhausted, and he fell to the ground without moving. Mortus laughed, and the battle stopped. All the inhabitants of the world of dreams looked at him in horror.

"Now the world of dreams belongs to me!" said the evil spirit, towering over them.

He put on the locket and turned to Peter.

"Come to me, my boy!"

But Peter shook his head, taking his sister by the hand.

"I will never do what you say again!" he replied.

"Ah, well! You chose the wrong side, so you will never return to your world!"

With these words, Mortus surrounded Peter with ghosts.

Illusius lay on the ground unconscious.

Mortus rejoiced, creating terrifying dreams.

Gladys ran up to the Dreammaker and shook him by the shoulders.

"Illusius, wake up! she pleaded. "You are a descendant of the Tall People and are able to create great dreams even without a medallion!"

Illusius opened his eyes, but they were filled with despair.

"Alas, I am no longer capable of anything," he replied.

"No, that can't be true! I did not lose hope," said Gladys.

At that moment, something unexpected happened to everyone.

Little Maya picked up a pebble and threw it at the crystal dancer. The girl froze for a moment and then shattered into hundreds of fragments.

"Oh no!" Illusius exclaimed so loudly that the whole world shook at the sound of his voice.

He raised his hands, and all the forces of the Dream World, both light and dark, began to flock to him. Mortus, along with the army of ghosts, dissolved and disappeared. Everything around was flooded with endless darkness, in which only Gladys, Peter, and Maya remained. The shard of time was the only source of light.

"What's happening?" Gladys asked fearfully.

"I think I understand," Peter said sadly, "because we all quarrelled too often, the world was swallowed up by darkness. And now we can never go back."

Gladys sighed.

"Let us promise that we will never quarrel and fight again."

"Let's."

The children hugged.

"How can we make the world the way it was before," Gladys asked. "When dad and mom were at home, and there was no destruction?"

"I don't know," Peter said with a sob.

Maya picked up a shard of time and, looking into it, made a joyful sound.

It reflected the erlins, the same ones who sprinkled the children with stardust. Jolo was among them.

"The erlins chose you for a reason," he said.

Peter and Gladys looked at each other.

"You, like other children of the world, have the power of imagination to change reality. And that is exactly what is required of you now. The way you imagine the world is the way it will become."

Gladys and Peter closed their eyes.

"Let's imagine," said the boy, "that the destruction in the world has stopped."

They tried so hard that the darkness around them began to lighten.

"Also, Mom and Dad are back," Gladys said.

"And the crystal girl on the rope came to life," said Peter.

"And that Tobo was free."

"And that the children of Sunfield went back to their parents."

And the more they imagined, the brighter it became around. Maya clapped her hands happily. And soon, the whole world around was flooded with endless light. Illusius appeared from it with a beautiful girl.

"She came to life," the Dreammaker exclaimed. "You helped me master the power of Mortus, and together, thanks to your imagination, we can create a new world."

With these words, he waved his hands, creating a huge whirlwind. A new, beautiful reality was emerging. The clock chimed.

Peter and Gladys looked at each other.

"Dawn," Peter said, "it's already here."

But before Gladys had time to answer him, everything dissolved, and they fell into a deep sleep.

Chapter 7

Return

When Gladys opened her eyes, she found herself lying in her bed in their house on Rose Street. Outside, dawn was just beginning to glimmer, and Peter and Maya were fast asleep, their noses buried in the pillows.

"So, I dreamed all this," the girl said, rubbing her eyes.

Suddenly, a whirlwind of cold air swept past her, and she noticed something white and translucent. It was Tobo, who was no longer chained.

"I'm free," he shouted, "I'm free!"

Peter woke up, rubbed his eyes, and immediately froze, staring at the ghost.

"Tobo, how nice to see you," said Gladys.

"I am free," the spirit repeated, "and it's all thanks to you! The children of Sunfield have found their parents again. Dream World is celebrating. Mortus dissolved and disappeared, Illusius controls everything now, and they say that the Dreammakers have returned to the city of Tall People! But the most amazing thing is that the portal to the Dream World will now be open every night! So come visit us whenever you want!"

And with these words, he sped off into the last remaining glimmer of night.

The children looked at each other happily. And when they went down to the dining room, they saw that their parents were waiting for them there. Dad made toast, and Mother poured tea.

"Mum, dad," Peter shouted happily, hugging them.

And little Maya squealed, clapping her hands.

Gladys was glad she met many friends and returned home unharmed with her brother and sister. But above all, this was a particularly joyful occasion for her because she discovered the Dream World and could always go back.

Thank you for reading a book from our project

and joining our journey in the Garden of Happy stories and adventures!
Audio books are also being introduced on our site.

Books are published in both English and Russian.

Dream World

WELCOME TO
THE HAPPY STORY GARDEN

https://thehappystorygarden.co.uk